D0230185

30131 05391353 6

Barnet Schools Libraries Resources Services	
30131 05391353 6	
Askews & Holts	12-Aug-2015
JF	£11.99

NOBODY'S PERFECT

David Elliott

ILLUSTRATED BY Sam Zuppardi

WALKER BOOKS
AND SUBSIDIARIES
LONDON · BOSTON · SYDNEY · AUCKLAND

"Nobody's perfect."

That's what everybody says.
And I guess they're right.

Like Gigi.
She's my sister.

She's not perfect.

She's loud!

Or my best friend, Jack.

He's kind of a show-off.
Not perfect!

And even my mum.

She put me
on the naughty step.
That's why I'm
sitting here ...

even though it's
not my fault that
Ralphie likes to sleep
on my bed.

I've told her a million times.
Ralphie should be put
on the naughty step.
Not me.

But she doesn't listen.
She's stubborn!

And
that's
not
perfect.

I'm not perfect, either.

This is my room
before I clean it.

This is my room
after I clean it.

But sometimes I *have* to be messy.

And sometimes it's fun
when Jack shows off.

And sometimes I'm happy
that Gigi is loud.

And even my mum.
Sometimes she does listen.

And when she does ...

it's perfect.

But sometimes
they come close ...

and that's perfect
enough for me.

To Susan Goodman, a perfect friend
D. E.

For Mum
S. Z.

First published 2015 by Walker Books Ltd
87 Vauxhall Walk, London SE11 5HJ

2 4 6 8 10 9 7 5 3 1

Text © 2015 David Elliott
Illustrations © 2015 Sam Zuppardi

The right of David Elliott and Sam Zuppardi to be identified
as author and illustrator respectively of this work has been asserted
by them in accordance with the Copyright, Designs and Patents Act 1988

This book has been typeset in Kosmik

Printed in China

All rights reserved. No part of this book may be reproduced, transmitted or
stored in an information retrieval system in any form or by any means,
graphic, electronic or mechanical, including photocopying, taping and
recording, without prior written permission from the publisher.

British Library Cataloguing in Publication Data: a catalogue
record for this book is available from the British Library

ISBN 978-1-4063-5944-2

www.walker.co.uk